The Case of the
Giant Gulping
Bluebells

Sherlock Hound

Make friends with the most famous dog detective in town!

Be sure to read:

The Case of the Disappearing Necklace

The Case of the Howling Armour

... and lots, lots more!

The Case of the Giant Gulping Bluebells

Karen Wallace
illustrated by Emma Damon

■SCHOLASTIC

To the Great Grimbly, who never gives up – K.W.

Scholastic Children's Books,
Commonwealth House, 1-19 New Oxford Street,
London, WC1A 1NU, UK
a division of Scholastic Ltd
London ~ New York ~ Toronto ~ Sydney ~ Auckland
Mexico City ~ New Delhi ~ Hong Kong

First published by Scholastic Ltd, 2002

Text copyright © Karen Wallace, 2002
Illustrations copyright © Emma Damon, 2002

ISBN 0 439 98102 6

Printed in Singapore by Tien Wah Press

10 9 8 7 6 5 4 3

The rights of Karen Wallace and Emma Damon to be identified as the author and
illustrator of this work respectively have been asserted by them in accordance with the
Copyright, Designs and Patents Act, 1988.

Chapter One

Sherlock Hound, famous dog detective, was crunching his breakfast bone when he heard two loud ringing noises. The first was his doorbell. The second was his telephone.

He picked up the
phone. "Yes,"
growled Sherlock
Hound fiercely.
If there was one
thing he hated,
it was being
disturbed at breakfast.

"Gertrude Greenfingers from next
door!" bellowed a voice.
"Something terrible
has happened.
I'm coming over
right away."

At that moment, Sherlock Hound's loyal friend, Dr WhatsUp Wombat, rushed into the room.

"Something terrible has happened," he gasped.

"My bluebells have disappeared!" shrieked Gertrude Greenfingers from the door.

Dr WhatsUp Wombat's eyes were as big as saucers. "So have all the Bank of England's bank managers!" he cried.

Sherlock Hound looked from one to the other. "Tell me exactly what is going on!" he ordered.

"Someone has kidnapped my bluebells," replied Gertrude Greenfingers. "And I've got to win the Greatest Greenfingers Competition this afternoon."

"Someone is kidnapping the Bank of England's bank managers," said Dr WhatsUp Wombat.

Sherlock Hound twitched his nose. It was a sure sign he was thinking hard. "Is there something extra-special about your bluebells, Miss Greenfingers?" he asked slowly.

"Yes!" cried Gertrude Greenfingers. "They're huge and they'll eat anything!"

"Return to your greenhouse, Miss Greenfingers," replied Sherlock Hound firmly. "I will need to speak to you later."

He crossed the room and put on his special travelling cloak. "Dr WhatsUp, we must go to the Bank of England right away!"

BANK OF ENGLAND

Dr WhatsUp Wombat gasped. "Do you think the missing bluebells have something to do with the missing bank managers?"

Sherlock Hound narrowed his eyes and looked suspicious.

"Who knows?" he replied. "But they both begin with 'b'."

Chapter Two

Two hours later, Sherlock Hound and
Dr WhatsUp Wombat had examined every
office in the Bank of England.

Each time, they found the same thing.

No bank manager and a handful of
bluebell petals!

"But how could a bluebell kidnap a bank manager?" cried Dr WhatsUp Wombat. "It's impossible!"

"Nothing's impossible," muttered Sherlock Hound. "Some things are stranger than others."

He took out his extra-powerful magnifying glass and peered at the carpet.

"Just as I thought!" cried the great dog detective. "Hairs!"

"What's strange about hairs?" asked Dr WhatsUp Wombat. "Hairs are everywhere. I found one in my soup yesterday."

Sherlock Hound stood up and looked serious. "Not a yellow hair with black spots on it," he replied.

"Professor Ha-ha Hyena," croaked Dr WhatsUp Wombat.

"Exactly, my dear Doctor," said Sherlock Hound. "Professor Ha-ha Hyena, master of disguise and the most evil criminal in the world." He picked up a handful of bluebell petals and stuffed them into his pocket.

"There's no time to lose! We must speak to Gertrude Greenfingers right away!"

Gertrude Greenfingers's greenhouse was very peculiar indeed.

As Sherlock Hound and Dr WhatsUp Wombat opened the door, two daffodils nipped their ankles while a geranium tried to nibble their ears.

At the end of the greenhouse, Gertrude Greenfingers was digging an enormous hole for one tiny tulip bulb.

"Madam," said Sherlock Hound in a serious voice, "I believe Professor Ha-ha Hyena has stolen your bluebells."

"Why would he want to do that?" cried Gertrude Greenfingers.

"Easy peasy," replied the great dog detective, pushing away a daisy that was trying to climb up his leg. "You said your bluebells would eat anything. I believe that the evil hyena is using them to kidnap the Bank of England's bank managers!"

"Impossible!" replied Gertrude Greenfingers. "My giant bluebells would never do such a thing."

"Nothing's impossible," said Sherlock Hound for the second time that day. "I'm afraid Professor Ha-ha Hyena can make anyone or anything do whatever he wants."

Chapter Three

Inside a dingy warehouse, Professor Ha-ha Hyena whistled a merry tune as he pushed two huge curly flowers on a trolley. It was as if he didn't notice the pinstriped trouser legs that poked out from among the petals!

Professor Ha-ha Hyena stopped his trolley. Then he pulled out a shiny red whistle and blew hard.

"Bluebells! BURP!" he ordered.

And as if they had been trained especially, both plants burped loudly!

Two men in pinstriped suits, carrying briefcases, shot into the air. They somersaulted once and landed upright on two padded chairs that sat in front of a thick wide curtain.

"Good work, bluebells!" cried Professor Ha-ha Hyena.

He dug into a bag of Meaty Chunks and gave each plant a big lump.

Both plants burped happily.

Meaty
Chunks

"You'll never get away with this!" shouted the men in the pinstriped suits. "As bank managers of a Very Important Bank—"

"You are getting sleepy," interrupted Professor Ha-ha Hyena in a strange soft voice. "Very, very sleepy." He leant forward and his eyes seemed to spin like windmills.

Then he pulled a cord and the curtains parted. Suddenly the two bank managers were surrounded by rows and rows of more bank managers! They all had a funny look in their eyes and they were all saying the same thing.

Professor Ha-ha Hyena threw back his head and howled with laughter.

"How-whoooo's a clever hyena?" he cried.

And he lifted a giant bluebell on to the
trolley and pushed it out of the door.

"Just one more bank manager!" cried the
evil hyena. "Then I'll be able to get all the
money I want!"

Chapter Four

Sherlock Hound stood in an office in the Bank of England. Except he didn't look like a dog detective any more, he looked like a bank manager.

Dr WhatsUp Wombat and Gertrude Greenfingers couldn't believe their eyes!

"What happens if something goes wrong?" asked Dr WhatsUp Wombat in a worried voice. "What happens if we can't find you?"

"What happens if we can't find my bluebells?" cried Gertrude Greenfingers.

"Nothing will go wrong," replied Sherlock Hound.

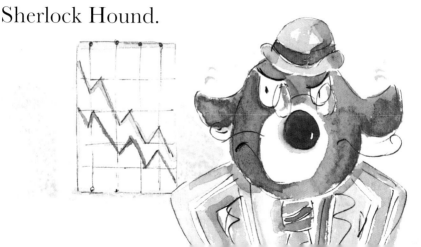

The great dog detective had worked out a cunning plan!

Disguised as a bank manager, he would get himself kidnapped, rescue the stolen bank managers, find the giant bluebells and bring the evil professor to justice at last!

Sherlock Hound held up a shiny brown sweet. "And the reason nothing will go wrong is because I shall swallow this tracking-device chocolate drop, then you will know exactly where to find me!"

"But chocolate *melts*!" cried Dr WhatsUp Wombat.

"It's not made of *real* chocolate," said Sherlock Hound in a patient voice.

He handed his loyal assistant something that looked like a tube of sweeties.

"And this isn't a real tube of sweeties. It's a signal finder."

Sherlock Hound swallowed the chocolate drop. "Now you will always know where I am!"

Five minutes later, Sherlock Hound sat at the big wooden desk in the bank manager's office. Suddenly the door opened and someone in a black and yellow overall, wearing a balaclava helmet, pushed a huge looselywrapped parcel into the room.

"Special Delivery!" said a muffled voice. Then the door slammed shut.

Sherlock Hound stood up and stared at the blue petals that poked out of the brown paper parcel.

Even though he knew it was one of Gertrude Greenfingers's giant gulping bluebells, he couldn't believe it would swallow him. Then he heard a whistle blow.

The next minute everything went black!

Chapter Five

"Hold it steady!" bellowed Gertrude Greenfingers as she drove her little green van at top speed. "Now which way?"

Beside her, Dr WhatsUp Wombat clutched the signal-finder sweetie tube.

It blinked red for left then green for right. Then red for left.

"Left!" cried Dr WhatsUp Wombat. "Right! Left!"

Suddenly the tube let out a loud BEEP!

Gertrude Greenfingers stopped the van outside a dingy warehouse.

"Madam," whispered Dr WhatsUp Wombat, "Professor Ha-ha Hyena is a dangerous criminal. I must warn you to be very, very careful."

Inside the warehouse, Professor Ha-ha Hyena sang happily at the top of his voice.

Everything was working out perfectly. Soon, he would release all his hypnotized bank managers back into the world. And then whenever he needed money…

The evil professor let out a howl of blood-curdling laughter.

All he had to do was ask!

Professor Ha-ha
Hyena blew his
shiny red whistle.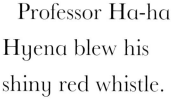

"Bluebell! BURP!"
he ordered.

Just as before, the
bluebell burped loudly!

Only this time, Sherlock Hound flew into
the air and threw off his disguise.

The great dog detective landed with a thump.

Immediately he noticed the bank managers were under some kind of spell. Sherlock Hound snapped his fingers. "Get up and go!" he shouted.

Professor Ha-ha Hyena roared with fury. "You can't do that! They're mine!" He climbed up the curtain and tried to fix the bank managers with his evil eye. But it was too late!

In one smooth movement, all the bank managers jumped up and looked at their watches.

"Goodness me!" they cried. "Is that the time? I'll be late for work!"

They rushed out of the room just as
Gertrude Greenfingers and Dr WhatsUp
Wombat rushed in.

"Catch that criminal!"
barked Sherlock
Hound. "Set the
bluebells on him!"

"Darlings!" bellowed
Gertrude Greenfingers.
"Come to Mummy!"
   The moment the giant
bluebells heard the sound
of their mistress's voice, they went berserk
and snapped at the first thing they saw ...
Dr WhatsUp Wombat!

While Sherlock Hound struggled to pull his loyal assistant free, Professor Ha-ha Hyena grabbed the curtain cord and swung across the room.

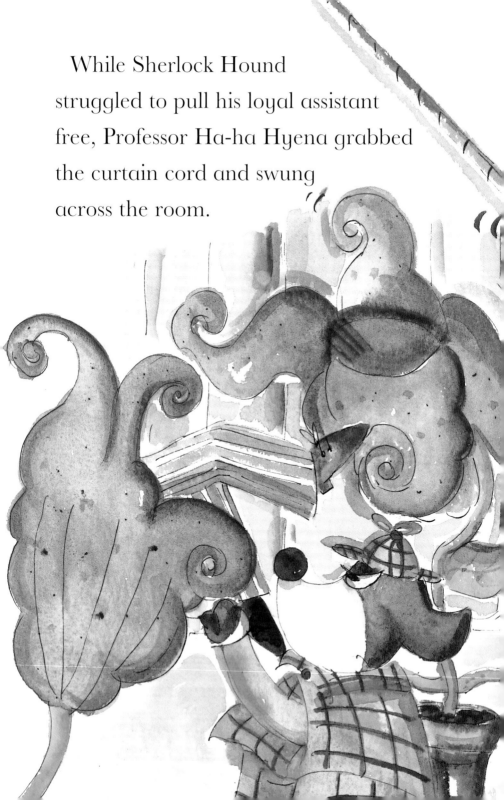

"You'll never catch me now, you flea-
bitten mongrel," he yelled.

And the evil hyena flew through the
open door!

Back at 221b Barker Street, Dr WhatsUp
Wombat was pouring tea when there was a
knock at the door.

"Special Delivery!" A young man
handed over a huge bunch of flowers.

"They're from Gertrude Greenfingers," said Sherlock Hound. He read the note pinned to the wrapping.

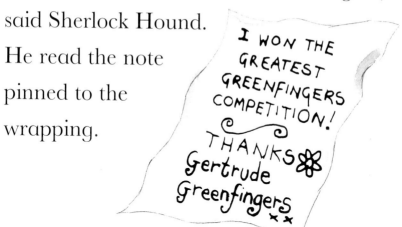

I WON THE GREATEST GREENFINGERS COMPETITION!

THANKS
Gertrude
Greenfingers
xx

At the thought of Gertrude Greenfingers's huge hungry flowers, Dr WhatsUp Wombat shook so much, the cup of tea rattled in his hand.

"If it hadn't been for those flowers—"
he cried.

"My dear Dr WhatsUp," interrupted
Sherlock Hound, gently. "The evil hyena
knows we are after him. Next time he won't
be so lucky."